Franklin Is Bossy

For the Pal family, especially
Katie, Charles and Stephanie,
because they love stories — PB

To Kerri Allen, a really good
sport — BC

0-590-47757-9

40 39 38 37 36 35 34 33 32 31   1 2 3

Franklin Is Bossy

Written by Paulette Bourgeois
Illustrated by Brenda Clark

SCHOLASTIC INC.
New York Toronto London Auckland Sydney

FRANKLIN the turtle could zip zippers and button buttons. He could count by twos and tie his shoes. He had lots of friends and one best friend, named Bear. They played tag and marbles, hopscotch and ball. But one day something awful happened. Franklin and Bear had a fight.

It was a steamy summer morning. Franklin told his friends, "Let's play marbles." And they did.

After a while, Franklin said, "I'm tired of marbles, let's have a race."

"You always pick the games," grumbled Bear. Franklin paid no attention.

They started to run. Bear was in the lead. Goose followed close behind. Franklin saw that he was losing and cried out ...

"Slowest one wins!" as he crawled across the finish line last.

"That's not fair," said Bear.

Franklin ignored him. "I'm tired of running, let's play baseball."

Bear did not put on his mitt. He did not put on his cap. He was mad.

"It's too hot. I don't want to play," said Bear.

"Me neither," said Beaver.

"It's not too hot!" said Franklin.

"Is too," said Bear.

"Is not," said Franklin.

"I don't want to play with you, Franklin!" shouted Bear.

"And I don't want to play with you, either!" Franklin shouted back.

Franklin stomped all the way home.

"What's wrong?" asked his father.

"There's no one to play with," answered Franklin.

"Maybe your friends will come by later," said Franklin's father.

"Maybe," he said.

In his room, Franklin built a castle. He made a cape to be brave in. He made shields and swords and suits of armor. He drew pictures. He played house. He read stories. He played by himself for one whole hour, and then he didn't know what to do.

So, Franklin went looking for company.
His friends were in the river, cooling off.
"Are you still hot?" he asked.
"No," they answered.
"Then let's play ball," said Franklin.

Before anyone had a chance to say a word,
Franklin started giving orders. "Bear, you play first
base. Goose and Beaver, you go to the outfield.
I'll be the pitcher."

"No way!" shouted Bear. "I don't want to play
with you. You are too bossy."

All of Franklin's friends nodded.

"Bear's right," they said.

Franklin turned his back and went home.

There was no one to play with and nothing much to do. So, he helped his father all afternoon. They weeded the garden and washed the floors. And they made supper for Mole because he was sick.

"You're a good friend," Mole told Franklin's father.

On the way home, Franklin asked, "Do you and Mole have fights?"

"Sometimes," said Franklin's father. "But we always make up."

Franklin played alone for another whole day. He missed Bear and all his friends. And he had lots of time to think.

He would go to Bear and apologize.

Franklin and Bear met on the bridge.

"I was going to your house," said Franklin.
"And I was going to your house," said Bear.
"I'm sorry," said Franklin. "It was all my fault."
"No, it was my fault," said Bear.
"Mine," said Franklin.
"No, mine," said Bear.

"STOP!" shouted Beaver, who was listening under the bridge.

"This is silly!" Beaver slapped her tail so hard that Franklin and Bear jumped. They started to giggle.

"Friends?" asked Franklin.
"Friends," said Bear.